Rita in the Deep Blue Sea

Iter
Th
is

Also by Hilda Offen in Happy Cat Books

Rita in the Deep Blue Sea

Hilda Offen

Happy Cat Books

For Sean and Niamh

Published by Happy Cat Books
An imprint of Catnip Publishing Ltd
Islington Business Centre
3-5 Islington High Street
London N1 9LQ

First published 2005
1 3 5 7 9 10 8 6 4 2

A CIP catalogue record for this book is available from the British Library

ISBN 1 905117 07 8

Printed in China by Midas Printing International Ltd

"It's nice to be somewhere hot for a change," said Mrs Potter.
"Where's Grandad? And Eddie and Julie and Jim?" asked Rita.
"Oh – they've gone for a boat ride," said Mrs Potter.
"I wanted to go!" cried Rita.
"You're too young," said Mrs Potter. "You stay here and do some paddling."

Rita watched the boat disappear over the horizon. Suddenly all the children in the sea started to cry. A big octopus had sneaked up and stolen their ice-creams.

"It's a good job I brought my Rescuer outfit," thought Rita.

She grabbed her beach-bag and ran behind
the wind-break. In the blink of an eye she'd
turned into Rita the Rescuer.
"Here I come!" she called and she dived into
the water.

Rita chased the octopus out to sea. Then she played a clever trick on him. Soon the octopus was tied in knots. Rita rolled him miles away from the shore.

"Please undo me!" begged the octopus.

"Only if you promise to behave yourself in future," said Rita.

"I promise! I promise!" cried the octopus.
So Rita untangled him. Just as she untied
the last knot something caught her eye.
A scuba diver had been trapped by a giant
clam. He struggled and struggled but it was
no use – he was caught fast.

Rita moved like a flash of light. She prised the clam apart and the scuba diver shot to the surface.

"Climb aboard, Rescuer," said a passing turtle. "I'll take you to the coral reef."

A glass-sided submarine glided by. The tourists inside stared and pointed. Just at that moment there was a juddering noise. The engine had broken down! Everyone started to panic.

Rita dived under the submarine and lifted it
above her head; then she carried it to the
surface.

The captain looked out.

"Can you mend the engine, Rescuer?" he
asked. So Rita grabbed a spanner and in no
time at all the submarine was on its way.

"I think you're needed on the sea-bed again, Rescuer," said the turtle. The scuba diver's friends were exploring the wreck of the Mary Jane. Oh no! They had been trapped by a giant eel.

Rita tickled the eel and it wriggled and giggled so much it let the divers go. It slithered away through a porthole.
"Uh-huh! Another job for the Rescuer," thought Rita, looking over her shoulder.

A swordfish was swimming towards a deep-sea diver; worse still, it was aiming straight for his air-line! Rita didn't waste a minute. She grabbed a piece of wood from the wreck and swam at the swordfish. Thud! She was just in the nick of time. The swordfish's sword stuck in the wood. Rita and the diver shook hands and the swordfish swam away.

Above them something blotted out the sunlight. It was a gigantic fish! It opened its mouth – and there, right above it, were Grandad, Eddie, Julie and Jim in their little boat.

"Must go!" said Rita.

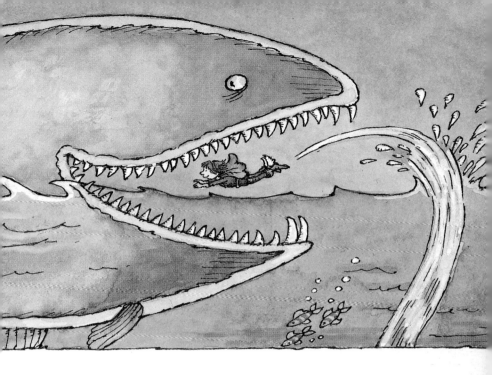

"Gulp!" The fish swallowed the boat whole.
There was no time to lose. Rita dived
straight in after them. She grabbed the boat
and pushed it out again. Then they whizzed
through the sea like a torpedo until they
were well out of harm's way. The fish flicked
its tail and dived to the bottom
of the ocean.

Rita felt something tickling her leg. It was a little mermaid.

"Hallo!" she said. "What can I do for you?"

"Please help us, Rescuer," said the mermaid. "A sea-monster has captured our treasure. He's sitting on it and he won't go away."

"We'll see about that!" said Rita.
Rita followed the mermaid to the mouth
of a cave. Inside they could see the sea-
monster glaring out at them. He'd caught
two mermaids and he was licking his lips.

"Yum! Yum!" said the monster.
"Let those mermaids go!" roared Rita.
She pointed her fingers at the monster
and zapped him with her sonic
shock-waves.

"Ow!" said the monster and the mermaids darted off.

Then Rita pulled a horrible face. The
monster was terrified. He gave a great
bubbly roar and swam away as fast as
he could.

"Oh, thank you, Rescuer!" cried the mermaids. They were so grateful they gave Rita a sparkly tiara from their treasure chest. "How kind!" said Rita. "But I must go. I'm needed somewhere else."

A giant sting-ray was about to attack some swimmers.
Whoosh! Rita grabbed the ray and carried it far out to sea.

After that she freed four little sea-horses who were trapped in a jam-jar. And last of all she untangled a dolphin who'd got caught in some fishing nets.

"Thanks, Rescuer," said the dolphin. "Would you like a lift?"
So Rita rode home on the dolphin's back and everyone cheered and clapped as they leaped over the waves.

"That was a good day's work," said Rita, and she zoomed up the beach. She darted behind the wind-break and changed back into little Rita Potter.

"We were swallowed by a whale!" called Julie, as the others leaped out of their boat.

"Oh dear!" said Mrs Potter.

"But it was alright," said Eddie, "because the Rescuer turned up and saved us."

"She always seems to be there when we need her," said Jim.

"Where did you get that tiara, Rita?" asked Julie.

"Oh – a mermaid gave it to me," said Rita; and everybody laughed.

Other Rita titles available in Happy Cat Paperbacks

Rita the Rescuer

When you are the youngest in the family, you can sometimes get left out of the fun. Then one day Rita Potter is sent a magical Rescuer's outfit which gives her amazing powers... Three cheers for Rita!

Rita in Wonderworld

Abandoned in the Chicks' Nest Play Area, Rita doesn't find Wonderworld much fun. Luckily she has her secret outfit to hand – soon she is tightrope walking, chasing gorillas and rescuing her brothers from a giant spider's web.

Rita and the Romans

Left behind in the Potter family's Wendy-house it is lucky Rita has her Rescuer's outfit to hand. In no time at all she's rescuing toddlers, saving gladiators and even building Adrian's Wall!

Rita and the Haunted House

Rita wants to go Trick or Treating with her brothers and sister, but they think it's too scary for her. Little do they know that she will turn into the Rescuer and do battle with *real* ghosts, monsters and a witch on a broomstick!